The bats come after supper . . .

slipping in through the window at the
top of the stairs. They loop through the
plants and up near the ceiling, hunting . . .
what? . . . we can't quite see . . .

then wheel back into the night. Bats.
Too busy, too careful to stay long.

The BAT IN THE BOOT

story and pictures by Annie Cannon

ORCHARD BOOKS   NEW YORK

It's Saturday. We clump into the mudroom from gardening, hungry for lunch. I'm making a place for my rake when something moves—something bumpy and rubbery and alive!

"A baby bat!" my brother yells.

"No, no, Catfish"

"You scared him, Will!" The baby is
disappearing backward like a rowboat,
using his wings for oars.

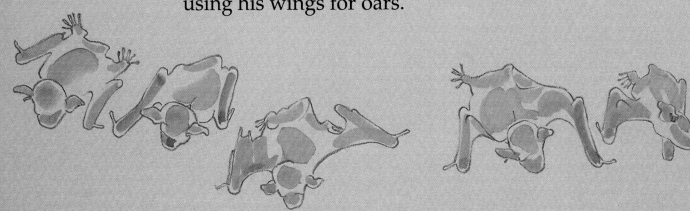

"*He's in your boot, Dad,*" Will whispers,
almost as loudly as he yelled.

We try to shake him gently into a shoe box. But he won't shake! On the end of each toe is a needle-sharp claw, hooked into the boot.

Carefully I pry him loose, toe by toe.

"What do we do now?" Will asks. "Hunt mosquitoes?"

"I think he's still young enough to nurse,"
Mom says. We warm some milk. The baby
ignores the spoon.

Mom tries a twisted napkin. The baby
sneezes and milk leaks down his chin.

Aha!

← milk
showing
through

"Remember the baby squirrel?" I ask.
"We used an eyedropper."

The baby's stomach is bulging and he's sound asleep. "Now how about *our* lunch?" Mom asks.

We set the shoe box high on the piano in the living room.

"Bats in the mudroom . . . a bat in my *boot*! I thought
bats kept their babies in caves," Dad says.

"Maybe the mother bats move them," I say, "like
Catfish moves her kittens."

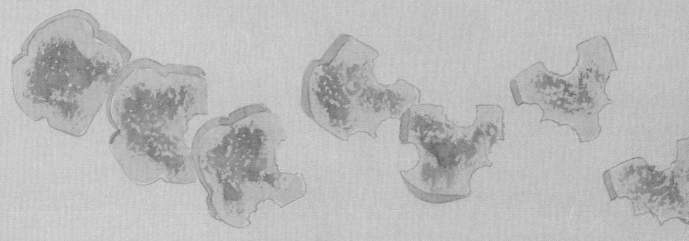

"Yeah!" Will says. "And she got hungry on the way, and flew in for a mosquito and forgot she was carrying her baby and opened her mouth and . . . *floop*!"

"How could she forget a baby in her mouth?"
I ask Will.

"Well, she *must* have forgotten him," he says,
"or where *is* she?"

Maybe something got her, I'm thinking.
Maybe an owl. Maybe . . .

"Mom, do you think the baby bat's going
to be all right?"
"An appetite's a good sign, Lilly," she says.

ch-i-i-i-i

All afternoon we're busy with the bat. One dropperful and his eyes droop. It seems like minutes later he's chittering for more.

"When's he going to learn to fly . . . and catch his own food?" Will wants to know.

Dad gently stretches out a wing. The bones feel rubbery and soft. "Not for a while, I'm afraid."

After supper Will wants to work on a picture puzzle. We spread it out under the window in the hallway upstairs. Soon it's getting too dark to see. The shoe box begins its chittering. I sigh.
"First call for dessert."

But before we can move, a large bat streaks
through the window and down the stairs. She
flashes back and forth above the piano. Suddenly
she whistles.

The shoe box squeaks.

"Mom," I whisper. "Mom . . . Dad . . ."

Will and I start down the stairs. The big bat spirals
up. We freeze. She flits about, hovering above us. We
ease the lid off the shoe box and creep back up the stairs.
Mom and Dad crouch with us at the railing.

Chirps from the box. The big bat zigs. And zags.
She dives straight in. We try to see, but everything
is shadows. We try to hear, but even the rustling
has stopped.

Then out of the darkness the big bat is flying upward. She dips her wings, cuts a hairpin turn . . . and she's gone.

We run down the stairs.

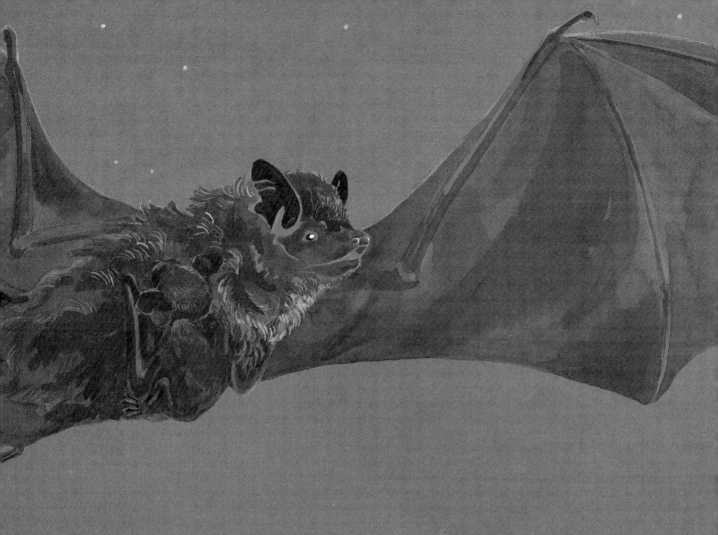

The shoe box is empty!

BAT LUCK

After that day we told everyone we knew about the bat in the boot.

"You're lucky," a zookeeper friend said. "You've seen something very few people ever will. But maybe that's not so surprising. In China people believe bats bring good luck!"

"It's lucky for us they like mosquitoes," I said.

"Yes—and stinkbugs and cucumber beetles! You're lucky to have found a healthy bat too," she went on. "Picking up a wild animal can be risky."

"But the bat in the boot was lucky we found him," Will said.

"Yes, he was," she agreed. "You kept him warm and protected him from Catfish. You helped his mom rescue him! Did you know a baby bat needs bat milk to survive? Now he'll grow strong—and he'll have other bats to teach him to hunt and keep him company for the next twenty years!"

The bats still come after supper.

We try to guess which is the bat in the boot, grown up now.

We think we know.
He dips his wings.
We bow.

For the Hilsmans

The Bat in the Boot is based on the true story of a real baby bat found in a real boot—and his surprising rescue! It happened two summers after my friends built their house. But it could have happened anytime. It could be happening now.

Almost a thousand species of bats are known to man worldwide! Many wonderful books are now available that detail their remarkable lives and their importance to our economy. To the best of my knowledge, the bat in the boot was a baby Big Brown Bat.

The *wu-fu* symbol illustrated on the jacket back has been adopted as the logo of the world's foremost bat research and educational organization, Bat Conservation International. The author is grateful for their manuscript review and positive suggestions.

Many other individuals contributed to this book with information and models, criticism and encouragement. My thanks goes to all who were so helpful!

Copyright © 1996 by Annie Cannon. All rights reserved. No part of this book may be reproduced or transmitted in any form or by any means, electronic or mechanical, including photocopying, recording, or by any information storage or retrieval system, without permission in writing from the Publisher.

Orchard Books, 95 Madison Avenue, New York, NY 10016

Manufactured in the United States of America. Printed by Barton Press, Inc. Bound by Horowitz/Rae. Book design by Jean Krulis. The text of this book is set in 18 point Andover II. The illustrations are watercolor, tempera, and pencil reproduced in full color.

10 9 8 7 6 5 4 3 2 1

Library of Congress Cataloging-in-Publication Data. Cannon, Annie. The bat in the boot / story and pictures by Annie Cannon. p. cm. "A Richard Jackson book"—Half t.p. Summary: A family finds a baby bat in their mudroom and takes care of him until his mother comes back for him. ISBN 0-531-09495-2. — ISBN 0-531-08795-6 (lib. bdg.) [1. Bats—Fiction. 2. Wildlife rescue—Fiction.] I. Title. PZ7.C17136Bat 1996 [E]—dc20 95-20849